Unleashed

THE POWER TO DO

MORE WITH ~~LESS~~ *MORE*

Tamara Sicard

CANDESCENCE MEDIA

tammy.sicard@candescencemedia.com

www.CandescenceMedia.com
info@candescencemedia.com

Quantity sales. Special discounts available on quantity purchases by corporations, associations, and others. For details, contact the "Special Sales Department" at the address above.

Unleashed: The Power to Do More With More/ Tamara Sicard. -- 1st ed.

Cover design and illustrations: Carolyn Sexton
Interior design: Gayle Evers

ISBN 978-0-9900219-5-7

Acknowledgements

It was April 1993 when I read a book that opened my eyes to a whole new way of thinking about organizations and the people in them. The book was *Leadership and the New Science* by Margaret J. Wheatley. Since that time I have been fascinated by ideas that shape our thinking about organizations, and what makes them work—not just for organizations but for the people in them. And I have been on a journey to discover my own part in helping leaders and their teams to engage people more effectively and more deeply in the reciprocal dance of individual and organizational thriving.

As my friend Jill Janov says, we stand on many shoulders when we write a book. I am deeply aware of and grateful to so many great thinkers and writers whose work informed my own discovery. I have also been fortunate enough to stand on the shoulders of many dear friends and mentors who have given me guidance, support and courage along the way. Jill Janov, Dr. Christal Daehnert, Maggie Moore Alexander and Sharon Gruber—you have each suffered through years of iteration, and your deep presence and loving attention have been a reservoir of sanity on which I have drawn for years. You will, no doubt, each see your ideas reflected in these pages. Linda Brown, Dr. Betsy Cole, Dr. Eleanor Scott Meyers, Dr. Rick Eigenbrod, and

Doug and Mary Fletcher, thank you for your insights, encouragement and good thinking from the very beginning. To my first mentors, my parents, thank you for a lifetime of love and support.

I want also express my deep appreciation to Dick Holm, who took me through the process of turning my ideas into a book. Dick, you are more than a great editor, you are a storyteller and magician! To my team at Candescence Media—Linda Alvarez, Gayle Evers, and Carolyn Sexton—you are creative and oh so competent. I am fortunate to have landed in your care.

And to my dear friends, colleagues and clients who took the time to read the manuscript, often more than once: Dr. Susan Beers, Sherry Benjamins, Bob Byrnes, Ric Franzi, Barry Hudson, Suzanne Middelburg, Lisa Rubino, Don Sciore, Susan Skara, Sharon Solomon, Karen Wales, Paul Wright, and Andrea Young. And to Tom Turnley—not only did you read everything I ever sent to you, you became my almost daily coach along the way, prodding and at times pushing me to get out of my own way.

And finally, to my steady, supportive, and spectacular partner in crime Sue Long for helping me in every way imaginable, both large and small, to stay with this long enough to see it through.

Contents

Section I

THE DILEMMA

Introduction

"Amid competitive pressures and a challenging global economy, 'doing more with less' has become somewhat of a battle cry for today's organizations."

—Mark Royal and Tom Agnew[1]

Organizations today are dealing with more of everything—more competition, more technology, more uncertainty and more change. The advantage belongs to those who can navigate this dynamic landscape better than their competitors. And they need to accomplish this amid constant pressure to "do more with less."

I have worked in and now with organizations for thirty years, and in each major engagement one challenge has persisted: how can leaders address the tension between functional excellence and cross-functional collaboration. Said differently, how might a leader get areas of expertise to

---

[1] http://www.bloomberg.com/bw/management/four-ways-to-do-more-with-less-really-11012011.html

2 • Tamara Sicard

focus on their part *and* do so in support of organization wide results—like profitability, customer satisfaction and quality.

When I ask executives what they believe is the number-one killer of competitive advantage, most say *silos*. Many feel that no matter what they do to get people to prioritize, communicate and collaborate across corporate functions, the conflicts, poor hand-offs, and turf battles continue. One executive commented that even at their best things seemed to be running on 6- rather than 8-cylinders.

When I ask employees what their number-one frustration is, they too say *silos,* though they often use different words to describe their frustration. Some describe their upset with another division that has created re-work for them. Others wax eloquent about the customer problems they have while they wait for information from another division; a division that is "not responsible for the customer."

When I ask middle managers *why* they think there are so many silos, I get a variety of responses: competing priorities; too much change; too much technology; isolated efforts; leaders who won't cooperate; not enough resources, time, or talent to get the job done (having to do more with less). The usual consulting solution? Tear down the silos.

But hold on a minute. What are silos anyway? And why is everybody so ready to tear them down, or at least talk about tearing them down?

Literally, of course, silos are towers on farms where green crops are compressed and stored for silage. They're airtight and watertight, impervious to outside forces. But they're not immune to inside forces: the gases, formed during the fermentation process, that can explode with tremendous force. So, while they serve the very useful function of storing grain for livestock, they also can have deadly consequences.

The same is true for the metaphorical silos that form within so many organizations. They must be handled with care. They cannot be left unattended. But that doesn't mean they should be abandoned or become scapegoats for other, deeper problems that plague organizational health.

As organizations increase in size and complexity, the need for separate areas of expertise, clear roles and responsibilities, and measures of functional success are crucial to competitive advantage. But so too is cross-functional thinking, decision making, and action. Otherwise functions thrive while overall results, and customers, suffer.

I've seen plenty of examples of what happens when silos remain isolated from the big picture.

- A sales rep closes a deal only to find that the selected shipping company used different specs than those followed by the company's packaging department, and the shipment was refused.
- A billing department employee refuses to speak directly with a customer about a complex billing issue because "that's the call center's job."
- Accounts payable leaves a message for a patient who they do not yet realize died in their hospital weeks earlier, upsetting an already grieving family.

I'll bet you could add plenty of additional real-world examples.

Organizations need separate areas of expertise. But they also need those areas of expertise to work together to deliver both functional *and* organization-wide results. Organizations need both functional excellence *and* collective intelligence. Consistency *and* innovation. Separate responsibility *and* collective accountability. Clear roles *and* collaboration.

How can we prevent our organizations from becoming like the reality television show "Survivor?" People divided into tribes (think silos), find themselves isolated in the wilderness (think further and further from your customer and internal partners) as they compete in a series of challenges (think budgeting) for cash and other prizes (think compensation and status) and are progressively voted off the island (think downsizing).

We need to help people be more effective across silos. As companies make major investments in enterprise technology and reorganization, or simply look for ways to differentiate themselves in the marketplace, this imperative becomes much more critical to return on investment and managing risk.

What we *don't* need

*Another book that describes what leaders
or employees need to be good at*

What you won't find in these pages is another description of what we already know: that organizations need people who are comfortable with ambiguity and who accept accountability for organization-wide results. Or that we need inspiring, self-aware, self-managing leaders who are great delegators and communicators.

More experts, more technological solutions

There is no shortage of experts in the world. Name a problem in your organization, Google it or Bing it, and you will find countless "experts" and technological "solutions" at the ready. Silos, however, don't lend themselves to expert or tech solutions. Silos are simply areas where people think from a narrow or functional point of view when they should also think from a broader perspective. Cross functional engagement depends upon people working together *across* boundaries to create productive solutions. Dealing with this issue requires the people who do the work to understand the work from an organizational, not just functional, perspective. Don't get me wrong. Experts and innovative technology have their place, but rarely will these externally sourced solutions help people embrace the context and complexity or engage more fully in their work. In fact, engagement can be seriously compromised at the exact time when it is most needed.

What we do need

A fundamental shift in how we think
about our organizations and the people in them

What we need is more *organizing* and less *dividing*; and for people, more *thriving* and less *surviving*. Even as the pressure mounts to do more with less,

di·vide
1. a: to separate into two or more parts, areas, or groups **b:** to separate into categories or DIVISIONS
2. to become separated or disunited especially in opinion or interest

or·ga·nize
1. to form into a coherent unity or functioning whole : INTEGRATE
2. to arrange elements into a whole of interdependent parts

gaining competitive advantage actually requires people to develop a capacity to do more with *more* (of practically everything)—more technology, more competition, more ambiguity and more change. The purpose of this book is to offer organizations a framework for engaging people to unleash this capacity. Organizations today need people clearly focused on their part; but they also need people who see how their work is dependent upon and impacts the work of others to support a "functioning whole" and organization-wide results. When these connections are clear, we see people who naturally think, make decisions, and take action *across* boundaries to restore and maintain connections—connections that are vital to innovation and integration.

Here's the dilemma

- If we want innovation we need integration, because innovation happens when functional excellence meets collective intelligence.

- If we want integration we need awareness of interdependence, because integration is only possible when people can choose responsibility for their part and feel accountable to others for the success of the whole.

- If we want awareness of interdependence we need to understand boundaries, and how they can divide or connect people and work that belong together. The boundaries we draw to organize work into functions, regions, divisions, or layers must become *defining* lines; they must not create *dividing* lines that result in differences in priorities, needs, expectations, and goals. What we choose at the boundary of our differences does indeed make a difference.

What we intend to do is organize—to break work down into manageable chunks. This is intended to maximize efficiency and effectiveness. But when work that is divided into "manageable chunks" becomes disunited, functions begin to operate as if they are independent of any other. What remains is a series of disunited parts, often working at cross-purposes.

An invitation

This book is an invitation to create a tectonic shift in our organizational lives based on a very simple premise: *If we change the way we see our work, the work we see will change.*

It is an invitation to explore and understand the boundaries that *divide* rather than *connect* areas of expertise and then to transform those impermeable silos into an integrated, functioning whole.

It is an invitation to be bound not by tradition or hierarchy but by our awareness that accountability, creativity, and collaboration are functions of self-leadership. In today's organization that is everyone's job.

It is an invitation to laugh at ourselves when the blinders of conventional wisdom fall off, and we realize what we already knew:

- That collective results are more than the mere sum of functional parts
- That aggregation is a poor substitute for integration
- That people, not technology, will integrate your business

Finally, it is an invitation to leap with courage and conviction into the unknown to discover what is possible when we unleash performance on behalf of organization-wide results.

A confrontation

This book is a confrontation because it challenges each of us to *discover* what we choose to do at the boundaries of our differences—be they differences in priority, expertise, role, opinion, or culture—and to *understand* the difference that those choices make to results and relationships. This is not a theoretical dilemma. How we engage people, within the structures and processes at work, is a very concrete choice and is not without consequences. The boundaries that define separate areas of work often become barriers to shared results.

See if this looks familiar:

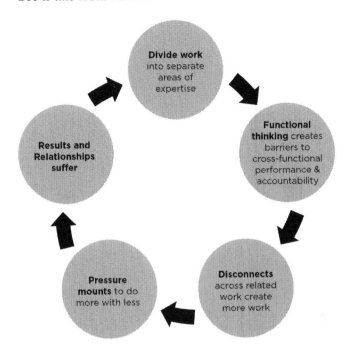

When we divide work that belongs together what grows is internal competition, poor handoffs, customer dissatisfaction, and employee frustration. Structure and process issues are misdiagnosed as people issues, and the pattern continues.

We must confront the reality that in an interdependent world, separate functions can turn into silos and result in fragmentation and isolation. Fragmentation leads to organizational suffering with hits to profitability, cycle time, customer satisfaction and quality; and isolation leads to human suffering—people looking for relief from frustration and stress because they don't know what to do to effectively address the isolation. Silos disrupt performance and accountability not because we have deep areas of expertise, or because people are not collaborative enough, but because the thinking within silos becomes isolated from other areas of expertise on which organization-wide results, and functional success, depend. In many instances, the cost of fragmentation increases with each strategic initiative that aims to do more with less.

Fragmentation demands that each of us confront how we think about and respond to chronic pressures of organizational life, and how we each can choose either to reinforce or to interrupt the repeating cycles of fragmentation and isolation.

A call to action

This book is a challenge—a call to improve the quality of thinking, decision making, and action across organizational boundaries by providing the structure and process to do so.

It is a call to engage your organization in what I have come to call the Five Decisions™—a framework and process to:

- Ensure *purpose* is both actionable and meaningful.
- Establish *connections* that matter to results and relationships.
- Make trade-off *decisions* to optimize overall results.
- Use disruptions and disconnects as opportunities to *develop capacity* for self-leadership.
- *Unleash performance* to drive organization-wide results.

Now is the time to dedicate ourselves to the possibility that some part of our chaotic and complicated organizational lives is the result of our own doing.

And then to do something about it.

CHAPTER 1

Silos at Work:
Technology Rich or
Technology Ravaged

"Technology is a queer thing. It brings you gifts with one hand, and stabs you in the back with the other."

—C.P. Snow[2]

We spend a lot of money on technology, often expecting it to solve problems that it can't. Technology can serve as a powerful source of competitive advantage when people understand how to use it to improve cross-functional results and relationships. But it can also become a beast that consumes time, talent, money, and morale when it is used *by* silos to work solely *within* silos. More technology will not eliminate silos; but technology can help organizations see where organizational boundaries divide work that actually

---

[2] The Two Cultures & A Second Look: An Expanded Version of The Two Cultures and the Scientific Revolution

belongs together. Why? Because technology sees across the organization; it is agnostic to the structures, processes, and customary practices that form silos at work. Take a look.

The project began in 2006 as an enterprise software initiative that started out like so many others. I had been retained to help a division at a leading global media and entertainment company get ready for go-live. They had only a few short months remaining, and the operational issues and challenges were giving team members insomnia. The team shared a nervous but familiar chuckle as one person said that he kept waking up with "one more thing that needed to be done" before go-live.

The people losing the most sleep were those responsible for master data.[3] This was not surprising since accurate and timely master data is required for just about everything—for the planning department to plan, the finance department to track costs, the sales department to enter sales orders, and the shipping department to ship.

Animated discussions ensued as the team began to more fully understand what it would require to ensure 180 fields of master data were completed accurately and on time by multiple departments. One team member explained the problem to me.

> In our legacy systems everything was in separate and distinct functional systems, so each function could be carried out independently. For example, a purchase order could be entered without a bill of material. But in this new system the timing and

---

[3] Master data is the basic business and product data that is used across the entire organization (and its systems).

sequence of events is critical to our ability to ship product and receive revenue.

With just a couple of months before go-live, the team realized that in an effort to meet the timeline they had excluded critical partners from the project. Those same partners were going to have very little time to get on board; and if they did not, then the company's ability to create and ship product would be thrown into disarray.

How technology becomes a beast

This state of affairs is not unusual. Many C-suite executives—CEOs, CFOs, and CIOs with high expectations—have, in pursuing a technology "solution," unknowingly unleashed a technology beast that ravages their companies. Enthused about technology's ability to boost customer satisfaction, streamline processes, and increase agility and profitability, these executives have bitten the bullet, gained board approval, and invested heavily in new technology.

But in many cases, the new technology broke down. Not only did it fail to deliver new capabilities, it rendered the organization unable to do things the "old" way. Inventory piled up, customers cancelled orders, and morale sank. Technology that held the promise of transcending siloed thinking remained in its own silo.

A pointed example of this problem hit the news in December of 2013. According to the Wall Street Journal, Avon pulled the plug on a $125 million order-management software system when "their workforce voted with their feet and left in meaningful numbers." The 100-year-old company wanted to digitize the experience of ordering Avon products using an iPad in the field, but, as Avon CEO Sheri McCoy noted, "The degree of impact or change in the daily processes to representatives was significant." The system's *functionality* was there, but the *usability* was not. InformationWeek reported that the project was intended to go global but was halted after four years. They referenced the company's SEC filing in which the company reported that a pilot program deployed in Canada caused "significant business disruptions in the market and did not show a clear return on investment."

Unfortunately, stories like this are common—people working hard within their function, completely undone by the larger dynamic. The technology beast finds their organization's weaknesses in processes and structure, devours its investments in people and in technology, and destroys its best-laid plans.

Most organizational change efforts are either challenged or fail outright. The same is true for IT specific projects. The system that is supposed to improve competitive advantage and customer satisfaction becomes a monster that consumes money, time, customers, and creativity. Few executives would knowingly take this risk.

Risk and reward

Executives are not the only ones who think about risk and reward. Everyday employees, when facing a significant organizational change, ask themselves, "Is this an organization I can give myself to, or need to protect myself from?" Leaders see the results of employees' individual and collective answers to this question. When processes and people are not aligned with new technology, frustration rises amid daily demands. People's senses of competency, affiliation, familiarity, and value are upset.

The same is true with any major change that people experience as a threat to their personal or professional well-being. When organizational change triggers our "fight or flight" response, then our best thinking, relating, and decision making skills go right out the door. When something triggers a stress-induced response at the time when organizations need people to be collaborative, creative, resilient, and engaged, people begin to hunker down in their silos and retreat into survival mode, hoping that this too shall pass. Or they simply leave altogether.

When organizations set out to solve an operational problem with a technology solution—how to integrate the flow of information *across* an organization—two other things usually occur that can derail the process and the investment.

First, common barriers to integration are exposed. New technology can expose barriers to cross-functional thinking and decision making that senior leaders didn't know existed. For example:

- Silos of experts who do not understand how their work is connected to the work of others or to the customer, resulting in poor handoffs and hits to customer satisfaction

- Decision making that advances functional priorities at the expense of overall results
- Organizational structure, processes, and policies that reinforce silos and business as usual

There was a time when this sort of deep expertise and decisiveness was viewed as a strength. But technology investments that require information flow and integration across functions for a return cannot tolerate them. The manner in which they undermine profitability and efficiency becomes apparent in rather short order. To realize the benefits of new technology, say cloud-based solutions, the organization needs to be oriented toward a workflow view of work even as areas of expertise deepen.

Second, new technology means new problems. New technology can create new problems companies didn't have before. Enterprise technology is often based on industry-wide best practices that are expected to improve efficiencies and existing workflows. Once the functionality is in place it takes time to discover all the ways in which day-to-day workflows need to change. For instance:

- Existing approval processes may get bypassed because the new system drives decision making to the lowest possible level.
- Contract price changes may stall because they now have to go through a new master data function instead of the department previously responsible for that task.
- Sales orders get stuck until the customer-material information record finishes its update.

- Customer service can't communicate with customers on what to expect because some functions are still tracking critical information outside of the new system.

These two types of tech-related issues exacerbate the friction already present in any change event or effort. New problems brought to light cannot be solved when the organization is struggling with disconnects and barriers to operational integration.

Challenging conventional wisdom

Faced with increasing pressure to deliver a return on strategic investments, executives then seek to understand why frustration is so high and return is so low. They tend to accuse the usual suspects: (1) the complexity of the technology and (2) the degree of change and the apparent connection between the new functionality and poor adoption rates.

When an expensive system has been implemented and fails to deliver the required results, most organizations turn to change management. The goal? Identify pockets of resistance, define targets of change, and get people to buy in to the technology that promises change and transformation. What is supposed to create the motivation for that buy-in? A burning platform, a good answer to WIIFM[4], or leaders who create a strong sense of urgency about the need to create change or else.

---

[4] What's In It For Me

Unfortunately, this response is a common mistake. It reinforces the notion that these efforts are technology projects, which keeps technology in the role of master and relegates people to a position of serving the technology beast. The usual focus for change management is to get people and processes lined up with technology as if it is a technology project and not a business-transformation initiative. Strategic initiatives aimed at increased efficiency and effectiveness require that people, working in a functional, mobile or geographically-dispersed environment, understand their work as a part of an end-to-end workflow. As mobile and cloud solutions allow for a more dispersed and global workforce, people will need to understand the expanding number of connections impacting their day-to-day decisions and actions if they are to make use of technology to transform results.

As long as people and processes are expected to serve technology, the proverbial tail will continue to wag the dog.

Reimagining people, processes, and the role of technology

I have spent fifteen years consulting with corporations on how to realize a return on strategic initiatives by helping them unleash performance *across* silos and improve enterprise-wide efficiency and effectiveness. Technology is often an important element in such a strategy. However, I have found that when technology consumes an organization's ability to care for patients, ship product, or receive payments, the technology beast is not a *technology* problem at all. It's an *engagement* problem. That's because technology can't innovate or integrate areas of expertise. Only people can. The same is true for any major change initiative designed to improve competitive advantage.

Oftentimes organizations buy technology, or implement other strategic initiatives, believing it will change their business. One client hit the nail on the head when he said,

> There is a perception that technology alone will produce lots of beneficial changes. That is not true. If we don't also change our structure—how we make decisions, how we think—nothing will change and the technology's purpose will fail. Sitting down and discovering this with our partners is the path to understanding and commitment.

The true test of effective engagement is in results—employees working together to find new ways to align *their* processes and transform *their* customer interactions, aided by technology.

Without this fundamental shift in attention and focus, organizations run the risk of becoming technology ravaged. Customers, patients, and employees are overwhelmed by the technology beast—relentless as it devours their time and their talent. Our world of work is changing. The interdependencies that drive risk and return are more and more important even as they become less and less obvious. One reason I wrote this book is to help organizations that find themselves either in this situation or close to it.

"This is remarkable work!"

Here's how one media and entertainment giant was able to tame its technology beast.

By the end of 2½ days of intense, determined discussion, the project team had identified the ten most critical functional impacts that needed to be addressed across their areas of responsibility, and they created an integrated action plan to deliver shared results. Functions that heretofore had been arguing over their separate priorities and needs found a way to collaborate across their differences to produce an integrated plan. That plan would reduce risk and deliver the intended results from this investment in technology. The group had come together.

The walls of the conference space were covered with an end-to-end picture of the relationship between people, processes, and technology. People saw themselves and their work as connected in ways they never had before. They saw their role in the larger context, and how to use information to make better decisions, decisions that could transform *their* business. It's exciting and engaging when people see connections come alive. At one point the CFO from the holding company walked into the room, took a look around, and said, "I don't think anyone around here has ever held such a complete view of our business. This is remarkable work!"

The team's ability to collaborate across their process and make trade-off decisions that were best for the operation as a whole, combined with the new level of accountability they shared for their collective success, led to a successful go-live of the system.

It can be done.

CHAPTER 2

The Technology Beast is not a Technology Problem

"The parts can never be well unless the whole is well."

—Plato

Gallup's most recent State of the American Workplace Report proclaimed that 67 percent of American workers are disengaged and therefore less likely to be productive. That means only 33 percent of employees are engaged, which Gallup defines as "involved in, enthusiastic about, and committed to their work and contribute to their organizations in a positive manner."

Gallup places the cost to the US economy at between $450 billion and $550 billion each year in lost productivity because these employees are "more likely to steal from their companies, negatively influence their coworkers, miss work days, and drive customers away."

My own experience of employee engagement is quite different, and more optimistic. *The problem is not that so many employees are disengaged, it's that they are poorly engaged.* When we blame people and leaders for structural or process issues associated with silos, when we misdiagnose the issue as interpersonal or intrapersonal, we trigger fear and frustration. This misdiagnosis leaves people with one option: find a way to survive.

Exposing silos

Consider this. All of us have grown up in a post-Henry Ford world. Ford went from building a car in his garage, to hiring a team of people to build a car, to an assembly-line approach to building a car. As the organization grew, separate jobs on the assembly line became separate departments with separate goals and separate areas of expertise. This division of work was intended to increase speed and efficiency, and it worked.

Fast forward a hundred years. As organizations grow in size and complexity, the unintended consequence of our ongoing assembly-line approach to efficiency is silos. Because organizations today function (or try to) through a series of complex connections, silos actually decrease efficiency as separate departments or divisions continue to see success from their narrow perspectives. They even begin to compete with one another for limited resources.

The increase in complexity, combined with the inefficiency of silos, has caused organizations to turn to technology as the new source of speed and efficiency. The complexity of work can be made manageable by technology that integrates a wealth of information to speed decision making, support more effective interactions with customers, and help people improve profitability; but when we lay an integrated technology platform on top of an organization that thinks and operates in silos, that technology becomes disruptive. People who once thrived on their own now can't get their work done.

Such was the case with a large pharmaceutical company who hired me to help them understand why their cost of goods sold was on the rise since their software implementation. We convened representatives from each function in the process; everyone from Finance to the warehouse floor was there. Their big "aha" came when the group started asking questions about why and where they had to use their new handheld barcode scanners. Manufacturing floor employees asked, "Why do we have to scan every time we enter a room, move product out of a vault, and use a machine? It slows us down and is frustrating as hell." Then a warehouse worker summed it up. "Yeah, we get it. We have to scan every time we spit! But why?"

That's when a brave individual from Finance weighed in. "Well, I'm afraid *we* did that to you. We got pretty excited about the ability to track cost of goods sold at the level of detail we requested. We don't *have* to gather data at every one of those points to satisfy our requirements."

And so the real work of transformation began. People worked together across functions to make technology and process decisions that improved profitability and employee engagement. Unfortunately, in this case it was too late. That client walked away from a $100 million software solution before we could engage the rest of the core processes to realize a return on their investment. The company blamed the technology for being too complicated and started over with a different software solution.

The technology beast is not a technology problem

Technology is here to stay. But along with advances in technology comes the increasing complexity of work and the resulting need for people to be able to see issues and opportunities from an organization-wide perspective. Social networking, workforce mobility, and the cloud all require changes in how people are engaged across boundaries to achieve organizational results. The root issue under most failed change efforts is siloed thinking that continues unquestioned. We can look to any major change effort to see where boundaries that define the work of separate areas are misconstrued and poorly constructed. What is more, we create silos of separate expertise and then blame people for not being collaborative, or not being good enough leaders.

Organizations often acknowledge the importance of having employees who can collaborate, build trust, and be creative and innovative. Building this sort of individual and collective capacity to think, make decisions, and take action across internal and external boundaries is a challenge that must be met. Organizations need people to continuously look to improve processes, make decisions, and improve performance across functions.

To remain competitive in today's complex global economy, organizations still need strong areas of functional expertise. But rather than an assembly line of separate silos, organizations need to enable people to:

- Be keenly aware of and interested in how their work is connected
- Choose accountability for organization-wide results
- Perform as leaders regardless of their role.

The transformative role of technology, or any strategic change, lies in its power to unleash people to perform on behalf of the organization as a whole.

The technology beast—or any change beast for that matter—is not a technology problem at all. It is an *engagement* problem. Taming the beast requires people who continuously look to improve processes, make decisions, and improve performance *across* functions. Return on technology comes from people who understand how and why to use technology to create an integrated and functioning whole. The beast lurks in process and structural issues, and in how we think about work as separate and distinct.

If you have made a sizable strategic investment (in technology for example) and are still waiting to see a boost in profitability, productivity, and customer satisfaction, don't give up on your investment just yet. Your path to success can be defined, developed, and implemented to deliver organization-wide results.

To choose accountability and perform at their best, people need:

1. A shared *purpose* that creates a context for collaboration and commitment

2. An opportunity to understand how work is *connected* across boundaries

3. Skills to make *trade-off decisions* that benefit the whole (e.g., the ability to see multiple points of view and hold the tension of multiple possible solutions)

4. The ability to *remain engaged* and provide leadership in the face of disruptions and disconnects

5. A sense that they are *mutually dependent* upon others for individual and collective success, *and accountable* for their impact on results and relationships.

The next five chapters demonstrate the Five Decisions approach for unleashing performance and accountability using an organizing framework of Invitation, Confrontation, and Call to Action to help you discover and consider new ways of engaging people more effectively and to encourage you to take a High Road in doing so.

The late poet John O'Donohue once said, "The great questions never settle to sleep inside answers." Instead of thinking of this as a "how-to" book with prescribed answers, please think of it as a general guide that can broaden your perspective on what works and what doesn't, on what makes sense for your organization and what doesn't. My hope is that it helps you engage everyone in a better understanding of where potential is trapped or untapped within your organization and what can be done about it.

This begins with identifying:

• The parts of your structure that reinforce silos
• Areas where there is a need to connect people across processes

- Opportunities for cross-functional decision making and action

It also means establishing collaboration as a norm and addressing cross-functional issues in real time.

The Five Decisions approach provides a scaffolding on which people can move back and forth to discover the connections and disconnects that naturally occur in a dynamic environment. They also help uncover ways to build the capacity to collaborate as needed. It's a common-sense approach that can ultimately become common practice in your organization.

The Five Decisions Approach to Unleash Performance

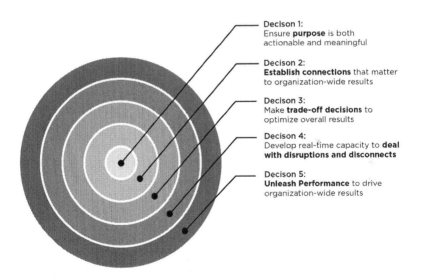

Decison 1:
Ensure **purpose** is both actionable and meaningful

Decison 2:
Establish connections that matter to organization-wide results

Decison 3:
Make **trade-off decisions** to optimize overall results

Decison 4:
Develop real-time capacity to **deal with disruptions and disconnects**

Decison 5:
Unleash Performance to drive organization-wide results

Section II

FIVE DECISIONS
THAT DRIVE ORGANIZATION-WIDE
PERFORMANCE AND ACCOUNTABILITY

CHAPTER 3

Decision #1: Determine purpose

"Effort and courage are not enough without purpose and direction."

—John F. Kennedy

The Invitation

"What is the purpose of my work?" This principal question needs to be answered and understood by both the organization that assigns the work and the individuals who undertake it.

From the organization's perspective, a well-stated purpose provides clarity and direction; it focuses people's efforts on accomplishing goals that contribute to enterprise results. Anyone reading a project or process statement of purpose should have a good idea of what the project will include and what it will accomplish. A clear purpose provides middle managers with what they need to bridge the strategic and the operational.

For individuals, purpose can create the *context* for collaboration, commitment, and accountability for collective results. Without collective purpose there can be no collective action; no reason to come together to solve complex issues; no sense of ownership to accomplish what none could accomplish alone. As individuals identify with something larger than they alone could accomplish, their work also becomes more meaningful as they identify with work that matters beyond their own small part. Who among us would not prefer to be seen for the positive impact we've had on others, and on results that make a difference to our end-users? When the work individuals identify with is bigger than what they can accomplish alone, they are far more likely to engage with one another to address issues on behalf of the enterprise rather than hunkering down in their own silos to accomplish their part and to hell with everyone else.

Purpose is a creative and energizing force. We know it is alive when we see people reach across areas of expertise to make sure a customer issue is addressed. But too often an organizational purpose is too large to be actionable, and a functional purpose is too narrow to engage people across boundaries to produce organization-wide results.

Purpose answers why. It does not come and go. As humans, we are always working on it. The question is, is that purpose large enough to help us provide something of value to customers and shareholders *and* meaning to our work lives? Also, are the conditions right to work on a larger purpose, or do they lead to merely surviving the tide, or tidal wave, of work that keeps coming our way?

I have come to believe, based on my consulting experiences with a wide range of companies, that we can't hold others accountable. Responsible, yes, but not accountable. Accountability is a personal choice. The question, says Peter Block, is "How do I engage people so they choose to be accountable?"[5] Accountability is powerful precisely because it comes from deep inside. But when an organization's focus is too small to allow or encourage a broader view, accountability suffers.

People treading narrow, dangerous corporate waters are consumed by staying afloat. A larger purpose, a swim, as it were, to a better place, remains an unfulfilled wish. And performance management, which often goes no further than assigning and assessing individual responsibility, fails to address the larger issues of purpose, both individual and corporate.

The Confrontation

So, what happens when organizational purpose doesn't answer why? What happens when instead of clarifying it confuses or contradicts? One result that I've seen is disengagement, not only from one's individual work but from the larger enterprise's. A purpose can be defined (perhaps unknowingly) to trigger Low Road behaviors:

---

[5]http://leadershipdiamond.blogspot.com/2008/03/peter-block-servant-leadership.html

competition where we need collaboration and conflict where we need cooperation and coordination. But when a purpose is clear and real (and maybe even inspiring), it can unleash the best people have to offer.

There are three main reasons, in my experience, why a statement of organizational, individual, or project purpose fails to engage the very people it's supposed to motivate.

The purpose is too small. It's hard to be engaged with work when our sense of purpose is so small as to make us feel small ourselves. We want to be part of something big, not necessarily in terms of its size, but in terms of its significance and relevance. If that something, or our role within it, doesn't have a larger purpose that makes us eager to engage with it, our best efforts might seem like a waste of time. Better to hunker down in our well-defended silos and hope for meaningful results and relationships there. After all, sometimes functional silos thrive while overall results suffer. Who's the winner then?

The purpose is too large. We also create barriers to effective engagement when our organizational or project purpose is too large and lofty to provide any real guidance. Again, major changes in technology, with all their tangled implications and unforeseen consequences, often put on display what can happen when the very size of the project becomes a problem in itself. A business case had to be made for the investment in the technology, so the organization's leaders have bought in. But what about the people who can't really see the link between their day-to-day roles and goals and the investment itself? Do they buy in? Or do they just give in?

The purpose is too idealized. Organizations often equate purpose with "vision statements." Vision statements became all the rage in the '90s, with everybody scrambling to figure out what the hell their "vision" really was and, assuming they did, how to turn it into words. It's not an easy process to create something that must get buy-in from senior management while ringing true with those charged with making the vision a reality. And because it's not easy, there's a tendency for vision statements to say nothing, really, or to become nothing more than part of a "branding strategy." Vision statements, if and when they're read, are especially problematic when they represent an idealized vision, one that has very little relevance to what people do and experience in their day-to-day organizational lives. When the reality that people experience is significantly different from the organization's vision, the vision becomes a source of cynicism and frustration. We call this a public-private divide. The larger the divide, the greater the cynicism.

Purpose can be more concrete and tangible than most visions, and more meaningful and inspiring than most goals and roles we "performance manage" around. When purpose is both meaningful and actionable it provides the context for collaboration and commitment.

The Call to Action[6]

Questions about individual purpose:

- Does my sense of purpose have meaning beyond earning a paycheck?
- Do I feel vital to the success of enterprise endeavors?
- Am I engaged in work that is large enough to create value or meaning? Do I see my work connected to the work of others outside of my area?
- Do I have the opportunity to learn, grow, and align myself with enterprise-wide efforts and results?
- What opportunity do I see to initiate cross-functional solutions?

Questions to ask about your organization's clarity of purpose:

- Is the organization's purpose a concept that people can relate to in their day-to-day decisions and actions?
- Does the organization identify and engage people in pockets of purpose necessary to achieve organizational outcomes instead of exclusively functional results?
- Do people define success in terms of isolated functional outcomes or in terms of enterprise results?
- Do people have the opportunity to come together to understand their work within the context of a larger outcome that none could accomplish alone?

---

[6] Download a worksheet with questions for all five decisions at www.partnershipadv.com

CHAPTER 4

Decision #2:
Determine connections

"Mastery does not mean having a plan for the whole, but having an awareness of the whole."

—Peter Senge, The Dance of Change

The Invitation

The world has grown smaller in terms of our access to each other and the impact such access has. Information traverses the globe at lightning speed. With ever greater sophistication, technology provides vehicles to reach people worlds away. And with economies tethered together by global commerce, a change in the Chinese economy can ripple throughout the global marketplace. Likewise, an environmental disaster in India can impact the rainfall in the Rocky Mountains. Political, social, and environmental boundaries have been rendered meaningless, as personal contact and technological integration have continued to make the world seem smaller.

But, in some ways, the world also feels larger. We can be neighbors and never meet. We can work for the same company, perhaps on the same product or service, and never see ourselves as working together. The world also feels larger when our differences polarize us. We can be in the same family, community, or church and find ourselves distraught over differences—political, philosophical, existential—that separate us and that the larger world confronts us with every day.

Yet we know that life depends on our connectedness. From the moment we are conceived to the moment we die, our lives are shaped by and sustained through our connectedness. Whether through an umbilical chord to our birth mother or a network of people who till the earth, we depend on our connections to sustain life.

We also depend upon strong connections for the smooth flow of ideas and information across our organizations. Connections facilitate engagement when people understand how their work is tied to the work of others—how it impacts others and is impacted by others' choices and actions.

When people are aware of the connections across separate but related areas of expertise, functional areas can act more in service of the customer and less in service of their own functions. And when connected people see the whole, they are more likely to call upon one another—to see issues and opportunities in a larger context as they develop the sense that they can (and really must) depend upon one another for their mutual success and that of the larger enterprise.

The Confrontation

Meanwhile, silos continue to isolate people and fragment work. And we can't act on connections we don't see. That's often why bright, capable, and seemingly dedicated people may do things that seem out of sync with what's happening in the rest of an organization. Or why, when changes and decisions that affect their work seem to suddenly come out of nowhere, they over-react. Or why they disengage entirely, only staying for their paychecks.

When work is conducted strictly within a silo, when connections are limited to others within that silo, a sense of isolation and dispiritedness can grow, unnoticed by others, perhaps, but always right there in the minds of those who feel it. It doesn't have to be this way.

Leaders and managers often attempt to provide clarity and direction by clarifying separate functional goals without understanding or articulating the connections between functions that can operate either to enhance or undermine shared results. Without this understanding, we cannot hope to get the needed performance and accountability required for organization-wide results.

Again, this is not a general indictment of silos. Many companies are organized to take full advantage of the benefits that silos or areas of expertise can offer. Consider the Cleveland Clinic, ranked by US New & World Report as one of the top five hospitals in the US. Its practice model hinges on three key strategies that organize work into a coherent and functioning whole that is at once separate and connected.

1. Specialists work as a unit to give every patient the best outcome and experience.

2. The clinic is organized into patient-centered institutes that combine the medical, surgical, and support functions for specific body systems or disorders.

3. All caregivers receive special training in empathy, communication, and caring.

We find silos no matter where we go—education systems, legal systems, political systems, business, healthcare—where experts go deeper and deeper into a specialty. In many cases, focused on their carefully articulated goals and roles, they are separated—even isolated—from others on whom their success depends. As knowledge within people's chosen field expands, somehow their worlds get smaller. Cross functionally achieved results, like integration and innovation, are even more challenging in institutions that reward those who specialize, as if each area's success was totally disconnected from others. And yet our usual answer when things get tough is to further define our separate roles and responsibilities.

In reality, connections, not divisions, are the organizing principle of today's forward-looking organizations. As they grow in size and complexity, they realize that an ability to connect across areas of expertise must also grow. A focus on organizational connections can help everyone become more business literate and involved. It can encourage and enhance opportunities for individuals to explore, express, create, and connect across differences and divisions to improve enterprise results. It can mean a fundamental shift in the structure of engagement—from divided to organized, from aggregated to integrated.

What kinds of connections are needed to deliver enterprise results?

- *People to people.* Through day-to-day conversations and routines that support information flow, individuals can better understand how to respond appropriately and come to grips with what's happening, even in the midst of uncertainty and ambiguity.
- *People to work.* Through a clear connection to the work at hand, people can see themselves as responsible for their part and be accountable for the success of the whole.
- *Work to work.* Through a bigger-picture understanding of organizational connections, people can be more effective across silos, building business and process literacy appropriate to the task at hand or the goal being pursued.

Here's what it sounded like as one leadership team I worked with began to recognize the connections between their areas of expertise and responsibilities:

> What we are discovering is that the whole process goes bankrupt when we operate in our silos, and that every one of us is critical; no one can be left behind in the process if we want to remain in business. We cannot succeed at our larger objective if each individual and each function doesn't find ways to connect our roles and responsibilities.

When I asked what difference they thought this sort of integrated thinking would make, they replied:

> We will make better business decisions. When we ask people to think about their work from a purely functional perspective they tend to make bad business decisions, usually without even knowing it. Our challenge is to figure out how to think about our business as a whole while we work from our functional perspectives.

When goals, roles, and responsibilities become disconnected from the whole of work, people naturally act within silos and "tend to make bad decisions without even knowing it." When this is allowed to persist, patterns of isolation and fragmentation become a reinforcing loop in which results and relationships suffer.

Imagine the utility bookkeeper whose job it is to recover unbilled revenue. The Bookkeeping Department prioritizes their work based on the amount of the bill—the higher the bill the higher the priority. The people in the field—on whom the bookkeeper depends to gather the data needed to create a new bill—prioritizes their work based on the number of meters they can read in one day. If a high bill is located in a remote area it may sit in limbo waiting for the person in the field to get to that location. If two weeks go by without a response from the field, the billing center employee sends a second request, which sits in their backlog as two backlog items rather than one. As the Billing Department's backlog of unresolved billing issues grows, the field remains successful in their priority—maximize the number of meters read in a day.

Doing more of the same in the billing department only adds to their workload, and to their frustration with the field. When functional areas of expertise achieve their goals in isolation of related departments, functions may meet *their* goals but overall results, and relationships, suffer.

Our individual and collective resolve to recognize and address the differences that divide people and work that belong together is a capacity that must be developed.

- -

The Call to Action[7]

Questions to ask about individual connectedness:

- Do I know with whom to connect and collaborate to support enterprise results?
- Are boundaries between my area and others supporting the smooth flow of information across areas of the business? Are they creating bridges or barriers to collaboration and coordinated decision making?
- Where can I forge stronger connections to improve results and relationships?

Questions to ask about organizational connectedness:

- Has the organization identified connections that matter to results and relationships?
- Is the organization providing opportunities for people from different areas or silos to get together to discover how their work is connected?

---

[7] Download a worksheet with questions for all five decisions at www.partnershipadv.com

- What functions need to be connected to deliver on the purpose and outcomes of a particular effort?
- What is the quality of the connections between these functions as measured by the results achieved and relationships established?
- Is there a strong enough technical and functional expertise?
- Is there a clear understanding of the whole effort to which each function is connected?
- Can we maximize functional expertise while simultaneously building literacy regarding the whole effort?

CHAPTER 5

Decision #3:
Determine trade-offs

"It has been taken as self-evident... that if everyone does his best then all will go well. But one of the most interesting things in the world is that this is not true... Collective responsibility is not a matter of adding but of interweaving. It is not a matter of aggregation but integration."

—Mary Parker Follett Prophet of Management:
A Celebration of Writings from the 1920s (p. 198).

The Invitation

Life is filled with trade-offs. We all need to compromise. Even the Rolling Stones can't always get what they want.

Rather than choosing between alternatives, trade-off decisions require looking at the bigger picture and evaluating alternatives that surface in the space between related functions, alternatives that are usually not evident from a functional point of view. A decision based on optimizing the whole may not sit well with all the separate parts that are affected by it, which isn't surprising. That's why it's so important to address trade-offs clearly and openly, keeping our eyes on the big picture even as we delve into the details.

Making smart trade-off decisions is perhaps the most difficult step in the Five Decisions process. Consider the organization that wants to drive down costs in its production processes and in doing so creates a quality problem in its product, which leads to an increase in customer complaints and the cancellation of orders. Some would say you can't have it all. You can't maximize profits, deliver exceptional quality in a timely fashion, and delight your customers. I would say that organizations cannot afford to choose between them. Quality, profitability, and customer satisfaction are not conflicting priorities or the responsibility of specific departments.

Rather than looking to the Quality Department, Production Control, and Customer Service respectively, these collective results are everyone's job. The ability to weigh functional ideas, issues and priorities from a collective point of view requires that we evaluate possibilities from an organizational point of reference while also contributing our functional point of view.

It's easy, and a big mistake, to frame trade-offs in terms of right thinking and wrong thinking, in terms of black-and-white questions and answers. Such an approach leads to decisions that lack the depth that a more expansive view can provide. A shift to the consideration of multiple possibilities, each with its upside and downside, opens new doors of exploration. Individuals exploring the advantages and disadvantages of each alternative can make trade-off decisions that are best for the whole, and then put plans in place to mitigate the risk or downside of their collective choice—this, as opposed to defending turf, competing for limited resources, or achieving separate goals without regard for the collective success.

Consider how functional areas of expertise have certain priorities on which they are expected to deliver and how those priorities often seem to be in conflict with other functional priorities. Quality trade-off decisions can only be made when these seemingly competing priorities are held loosely and weighed in relationship to one another in service of collective success.

The ability to hold not just a functional point of view but also a collective point of reference is a capacity that can be developed.

When people have the opportunity to explore competing priorities from a collective perspective—rather than a functional one—they can improve the quality of thinking, decision making, and action that serves enterprise results. They can innovate. The ability to recognize internal and external dynamics at play, to understand complex interrelationships and multiple perspectives, is a meaning-making process that bridges the individual and organizational to create accountability and performance.

This is also a choice.

The Confrontation

We've heard it so often that it's become a cliché: "Do more with less." Cliché or not, in today's highly competitive marketplace, there is unrelenting pressure of all kinds, most notably to increase revenues and decrease costs. Thus, the command, "Do more with less."

When companies adopt such a strategy, individual silos are charged with implementing it. In a fragmented organization, where boundaries that define work also divide work, the drive to do more with less leaves people with nowhere to turn except their own silos. So they hunker down there, isolating themselves from collective responsibility. Meanwhile, the organization continues to implement strategic changes to do more with less.

Some strategies are additive:

- Invest in new technology
- Acquire a company with complementary products
- Streamline processes
- Invest in R&D
- Innovate new products or customer solutions

Some are subtractive:

- Reduce budgets
- Reduce headcounts
- Eliminate less profitable lines of business
- Merge redundant functions
- Cancel projects

Rarely, however, are people in silos able to do more with more technology, more change, more ambiguity, and more uncertainty. This is because the trends, issues, and patterns surfacing across the business—driving costs up and quality and customer satisfaction down—are simply too complex to be addressed in silos.

As efforts fracture and fragment, poor hand-offs and disconnects across work result in higher costs, wasted resources, erosion of customer and shareholder value, and fear and frustration among employees who feel powerless amidst the pressure to address these costs of fragmentation. Functions struggle to survive as overall results, like innovation, suffer.

When organizations engage people in functional areas of expertise without a larger point of reference to guide them, silos form. When organizations engage people to explore, understand, and weigh their work across areas of expertise, they build a capacity for appreciating the bigger picture even while living with a certain amount of ambiguity. They do more with more.

There's something else that creates a barrier to collective results—our celebration of individual expertise.

In 1978, Genentech became the first biotechnology company when they successfully developed genetically engineered human insulin. Earlier in the 1970s, Harvard's own Walter Gilbert said biologists at some of our greatest academic institutions had, "an unspoken oath to do biology with an ivory-tower view and with no practical applications in mind." Genentech had a different idea. That idea was to bring together scientists from various specialties—molecular biologists, protein chemists, organic chemists, and the like. In just a few years Genentech would introduce the world to the first laboratory-produced human insulin. I asked one of the executives who helped lead the organization through this time how the Genentech team managed to beat Harvard—one the country's most prestigious academic institutions—to market. He credited Genentech's collaborative approach.

Bringing together scientists who worked in separate departments, and often in separate buildings, was what Gilbert and his team at Harvard could not do. Crossing boundaries in an established institution is far more difficult than in an entrepreneurial start up. Genentech would lead the way to create a brand new industry—biotechnology—an industry that is expected to exceed 200 billion US dollars by 2016. Oh, and one other thing happened in 1978. Walter Gilbert left his job at Harvard to cofound Biogen, which would soon write its own remarkable biotechnology success story.

In the high-pressure world of work, our ability to create a culture of performance and accountability is hampered when a focus on individuals and functional expertise is not balanced with an understanding of how each area is dependent upon others to deliver collective results. Trade-off decisions are one way to bring to light a fact of today's organizational challenges—the thinking, decision making, and action *across* efforts is the only way to achieve *collective* results.

The Call to Action[8]

Questions to ask about individual trade-offs:

- Do I look for solutions that are best for the business or do I compete to protect and defend my position?

Questions to ask about organizational trade-offs:

- Are there formal structures and processes in place that engage cross-functional collaboration and trade-off decisions?
- Have we driven decision making to the lowest possible level so that day-to-day trade-off issues are visible?
- Do people have the authority to surface and address these issues together?
- Is there any incentive to do so?
- Do people have the skills to navigate these seemingly competing priorities?

This last question brings us to the next conversation—how to deal effectively with the disconnects that are inevitable in cross-functional work.

---

[8] Download a worksheet with questions for all five decisions at www.partnershipadv.com

CHAPTER 6

Decision #4: Determine disconnects, develop collaborative leadership

"A true commitment to helping people grow is an act of faith. You have to believe in your heart that people want to pursue a vision that matters, that they want to contribute and be responsible for results, and that they are willing to look for shortfalls in their own behavior and correct problems whenever they are able. These beliefs are not easy for control-oriented managers, and that's why there remains a gap between the 'talk' and the 'walk' regarding developing people."

—Rich Teerlink, CEO Harley Davidson

The Invitation

Forward-looking organizations expect disruptions and disconnects and strive to see them as opportunities for improving and innovating, and, in the process, fostering collaborative leadership skills in those involved with finding and implementing solutions. Such organizations develop a capacity to identify and evaluate reactive versus creative responses. They're aware that when a cross-functional issue is being addressed from a reactive stance, the result is conflict and competition rather than collaboration. They also recognize that being able to step back, reflect, and choose one's response is basic to building a capacity for self-leadership, let alone leadership of others. They know that investing in personal and group capacity to deal effectively with differences, address disconnects, and respond to ambiguity will improve the quality of thinking, decision making, and action across all areas of expertise.

We need to continuously identify and address disconnects between people, processes, and technology as we operate in a dynamic and complex world. Individual and organizational factors that undermine performance and accountability must be surfaced. In taking on this ongoing task, organizations need to enlist the talents of their most valuable assets: the people who together make the whole effort work. Not just executives and managers, but all the people who are in positions that give them practical, realistic views of what's happening around them—people who have the desire to develop their capacity for self-leadership. People on the front line are usually the ones who can both investigate and capture the missing connections. When the connections are understood, solutions can be found.

The Confrontation

When the pressure and organizational demands trigger our survival mode, our best thinking and relating skills fly right out the window. We become reactive to the fear and frustration instead of engaged in addressing cross functional issues. We even see competition and conflict where what is needed is collaboration and coordinated action.

Consider how one pharmaceutical organization *divided* responsibilities between two *related* functions, resulting in fragmented work and frustrated people:

> **The situation:** As the head of Compliance, Megan answered internally to the Quality Department and externally to the FDA about the company's ability to account for controlled substances. As the head of Corporate Security, Jonathon reported to Engineering Operations regarding Security's plans and actions to secure facilities in which these substances were stored.

- When Megan would initiate an audit to ensure a particular secured facility was in compliance with FDA requirements Jonathon felt policed.
- When Jonathon would initiate changes to storage facilities in which these substances were housed Megan felt he had done an end-run around her.

> **The impact:** The conflict between them became personal, and it extended into their teams. People who needed to be collaborating to ensure FDA compliance—compliance that was a condition of their continued production of product—were in conflict.

The suggestion: Jonathon recommended that they further clarify their separate roles and responsibilities "...where the activities of Compliance and Corporate Security currently and/or potentially overlap."

This is a common mistake. When disconnects between related work occur, conventional wisdom leads us to further delineate responsibilities when what is needed are stronger connections between related work.

The solution: We agreed to engage a cross-functional project team to identify the interfaces needed between the two groups to ensure organization-wide success and FDA compliance.

Individuals and teams can develop the capacity to provide leadership in the midst of differences and disconnects. We call this collaborative leadership.

As author and speaker Meg Wheatley reminds us, "There are no recipes or formulae...There is only what we create through our engagement with others and with events." Collaborative leadership is a practice that improves our capacity to deal with others and events, and to remain engaged in the midst of differences and disconnects. It involves an ability to remain calm in the midst of ambiguity or stress, to get clear about the larger picture of what is going on, to remain curious and ask powerful questions that evoke curiosity and new insights, and to create an opening for creativity when it would be much easier to simply react.

The department chair position in universities is one of the most challenging roles I've observed. What makes it especially difficult is that while department chairs are responsible for coordinating and implementing a variety of projects, their position holds zero authority to make anything happen. Talk about having to work amid ambiguity and stress! And to make matters more challenging, once their term as chair is served, the professor is back in the role of colleague with peers who may not have appreciated the projects implemented under her watch.

When relationships and the goal or initiative are equally critical to success, collaborative leadership skills are key. Collaborative leadership is needed at all levels to:

- Solve problems that cut across the enterprise, impacting multiple people, functions, differences, needs, concerns, points of view, geographical regions, and overall culture
- Understand the complex nature of work and the challenges people face
- Connect people's expertise and knowledge with others and to larger organizational goals
- Remain focused on the enterprise as a whole

When conflicts arise, collaborative leaders walk a very fine and skillful line to deliver results while also preserving relationships. When differences arise, how we choose to respond does indeed make a difference.

The Call to Action[9]

Questions to ask about individual disconnects, and developing collaborative leadership:

- Do I provide collaborative leadership when we experience disconnects and disruptions, or do I react to these circumstances?
- How can I continue to remain curious in the midst of ambiguity and complexity instead of running for cover?
- How can I develop my capacity to solve problems that cut across the enterprise?
- How can I connect my expertise to goals larger than my own function or silo?
- How can I collaborate with others to keep our focus on the enterprise as a whole?
- Do I want to learn to do this work?

Questions to ask about organizational disconnects and collaborative leadership:

- What disconnects are obvious and need to be addressed?
- How do we become aware of fatal disconnects as we proceed?
- Is there enough organizational support to encourage routine identification of cross-functional issues and the development of self-leadership skills?

---

[9] Download a worksheet with questions for all five decisions at www.partnershipadv.com

- Do our investments in the growth and development of people help them work more effectively to solve cross-functional and complex issues?

CHAPTER 7

Decision #5:
Develop a sense
of belonging

"Ethics is how we behave when we decide we belong together."

—David Stendl Rast and Fritof Capra, Belonging to the Universe

----

The Invitation

Does belonging have a place in corporate life and leadership? A few organizations that I've worked with think so. They understand the transformative power of belonging. They know that when people feel they belong, they can grow and thrive. They know that when people work with others to identify and solve their own issues, they're empowered, no longer depending on people in positions of leadership to drive change. They know that inviting and engaging people to work together across areas of expertise, geography, and organizational levels generates collective awareness and accountability for the entire enterprise and not just functional excellence. They recognize this as a sure antidote to the fragmentation that silos can spawn and that most organizations struggle to understand and address.

And yet, we seldom see "belonging" cited as a crucial element of effective organizations, let alone used in the same sentence with "succeeding." Too often it's seen as "soft" and unmeasurable, like individual, personal, or family issues. "Hard" business issues, on the other hand, like cost, speed, profit, can be easily explained, quantified, and understood. As a result, soft issues, like belonging, are often relegated to a permanent place on the back burner. My experiences have convinced me that belonging should have a permanent place on the *front* burner.

Human beings share a need to belong—to feel they're part of the world they inhabit, part of something bigger than themselves. People everywhere strive for a sense of belonging to something beyond themselves—families, friends, communities, schools, clubs, social organizations. We know when we belong. We feel it. We feel exclusion, too, probably more often than we'd like to admit.

Belonging is a subject that social scientists, educators, and poll takers of various stripes research extensively. You can find all kinds of information about the role that a student's sense of belonging plays in academic achievement. You can find surveys measuring people's sense of involvement and acceptance in their communities, their sense of connection with a local sports team, or their allegiance to a political party.

But there's one central area of our lives where the significance of belonging receives little attention: our work lives. Try to find a magazine article ("Workers clueless about colleagues, roles, mission") or a research paper ("Belonging as a catalyst to innovation") about it. There's not much out there.

Maybe that's because, while we may worry about our kids' sense of belonging in school and elsewhere, we don't pay the same attention to our own need to belong as participants in businesses and other purposeful organizations. Neither do we, as leaders, pay the same attention to others—colleagues, direct reports, "subordinates"—and whether or not they may share the sense of belonging that we might try to instill in them.

A sense of belonging within our organizations is crucial to both personal and organizational success. Understanding our own impact on people and performance is the first step to effective engagement. As leaders, we must strengthen or restore our own sense of belonging so we can help others do the same. This is why leadership development *is* self-development.

A sense of belonging is what feeds our capacity to be self-reflective, embrace complexity, appreciate ambiguity and uncertainty, accept personal responsibility, hold multiple points of view, appreciate and enjoy personal differences, collaborate to improve productivity and resolve conflict, and remain open to creating new narratives.

The Confrontation

Not long ago I spent three days with one of the most remarkable group of leaders I have ever had the pleasure to work with. They are leaders who have the wealth, will, and reach to attain their goal of eliminating poverty around the world. Yet at the end of our time together I told them, "Working with you is like riding a horse that decides to stop just as we approach the jump together, sending me catapulting through space wondering what happened to my horse." The jump they aborted each time we approached? What Mary Parker Follett called *collective responsibility:* the choice-full ability to interweave and integrate rather than add and aggregate our efforts.

As powerful as this group of individuals was, their greatest potential for eliminating global poverty was in their *collective* power. Although they shared a vision to fight poverty, they remained 26 *individuals who never quite came together as a whole.* Each had something profound to contribute, but when I asked what was required of them together, the leap to a collective effort became a barrier that stopped them cold.

How could a group of such capable, resourceful, and well-intentioned people struggle to join one another in what they clearly could only address together? How could so much potential for shared performance and accountability be trapped in the space between them?

Addressing this challenge—striving to cultivate a stronger sense of belonging—gives us the opportunity to choose a new path. I call this path the High Road. We have a choice in how we meet the "Me versus Us" tensions that naturally arise between functions that have become divided. When we engage from our High Road we are more likely to maintain our cool when difficulties arise. On our High Road differences and disconnects are to be expected as we work together to improve performance and deliver organization-wide rather than functional results.

On our Low Road we are more reactive, and inclined to protect ourselves or our interests. We seek certainty and tend to simplify cross-functional issues into black and white, either-or thinking. Choosing our High Road as leaders not only restores us, it has the potential to restore relationships and improve results. It helps us become the kind of leaders who continuously strive to improve our impact on people and performance. It helps us become the kind of leaders we want to be.

To cultivate a stronger sense of belonging we need to develop:

- The ability to recognize own High Road and Low Road behaviors
- The capacity to step back, reflect, and choose a High Road response that serves both results and relationships
- The capacity to see beyond ourselves and our own views—softening our boundaries to discover a larger, fuller narrative
- The cross-functional initiative to invest in a task with others, especially when it's not our job to do so.

Our ability to recognize our internal response to differences, disconnects and disruptions, and then choose to engage from our High Road is a choice for accountability and performance. Each decision we face, and every choice we make, directly impacts our chances for successful change. Each is a step toward or away from the culture of performance and accountability we seek.

The Call to Action[10]

Questions for individual leaders and their impact on people and performance:

- How can I become more aware of my inner response before I act/react?
- What is my particular brand of Low Road behavior? What impact do I have on people? On performance?
- What is the gift I bring to the organization when I am at my best, operating from my High Road?
- What opportunities do I see to improve my impact on people and performance?

Questions for our organization and the impact of our environment on people and performance:

- Is our culture reactive or creative in the face of uncertainty and ambiguity?
- Do our change efforts trigger fear and frustration, or engage a sense of curiosity and creativity?

---

[10] Download a worksheet with questions for all five decisions at www.partnershipadv.com

- Do people demonstrate cross-functional initiative and partnership?
- The opposite of belonging is isolation. Where on the continuum of belonging and isolation do I see people in our organization and why?

Section III

CONCLUSION AND EPILOGUE

CHAPTER 8

How Thriving Organizations do More with ~~Less~~ *More*

"Work is where the self meets the world."

—David Whyte

It pained me to read a friend's recent note: "Project going well so far. Lots of the process mapping has been done. Very much driven by the consultants…"

It was great news up until that last sentence, "Very much driven by the consultants…"

Don't get me wrong; process mapping is integral to a successful implementation. But process mapping won't develop a culture of performance and accountability if it's performed by anyone other than the people responsible for the work. Why?

Engaging people to map their own processes produces results and rewards of its own. We engage people across silos to help them develop process literacy; to struggle with difficult trade-off decisions; and to overcome barriers to organization-wide performance and accountability. The *output* is a process map. But the changes in the new process map are secondary to the changes in how people think about their work and each other.

Changes in technology, structure, or strategy do not transform a business; people do. When we confuse these elements of organizational change we increase risk and decrease return on strategic investments.

The potential for doing more with more change, more technology, and more uncertainty increases when people:

• Know their process
• Know the purpose of the process
• Know their part within that process
• Know and manage themselves in the midst of uncertainty and change

An emphasis on change management and training will do little to increase the number of successful projects.

As long as our approach to engaging people is constrained by the same thinking that limits risk and reward to the tasks and transactions of a project plan, our efforts at engagement will fall short. Our efforts to create a culture of performance and accountability can succeed when we remember both the individual and the organizational; the tangible and the intangible. When we do this, the things we focus on change. We might catch ourselves in the old mindset, thinking about people as *targets of change* instead of partners and collaborators on whom a change effort depends. We might recognize that poor handoffs between functions are an *opportunity to improve connections* across functions—rather than to further define separate responsibilities. And we might address differences, disconnects, and disruptions as opportunities for collaborative leadership.

I can hear the objections now. "I don't have the time, the authority, the skills, or the luxury to engage people this way!" But this approach to engagement is *not* one more thing to add to an already overwhelming list of deliverables and timelines. It *is* disruptive to the conventional wisdom that sticks organizations in silos that create systemic barriers to integration, innovation, and a sense of interdependence.

Only human beings possess the curiosity to ask:

- How does this work?
- Where do I fit in?
- What does that change mean to me? To us?
- What difference does this make?
- What difference do I make?
- Why are we doing this?

When we deprive ourselves of the opportunity to explore these real questions that fuel a sense of belonging, we also deprive ourselves of the potential that comes with real engagement, engagement built on a sense of connection to others in work that matters. A true commitment to engagement is an act of faith in people. It is an act of courage.

A client of mine, a division vice president, was recently tasked with reducing her organization by half. It was a shocking directive, but given the changes in their industry it was also a necessary part of remaining competitive. Because the target was so high, she knew that reaching it would require a completely different operating model—and that a completely different operating model would require some very creative thinking. Thus began the work of engaging people in the difficult but necessary work of collaborating to design an uncertain future. Her deep faith in people was perhaps best reflected in the feedback from a leader in another division that would be impacted by her organizational changes:

> *Those folks have sand [by which he meant courage and tenacity]. I am humbled by the integrity and professionalism shown by your folks to engage us, and the lengths they are willing to go to ensure that this is a smooth transition, and that they are able to support the field as appropriate while facing the loss of their own jobs. Good folks, good partners. Proud to be on their crew.*

A culture of shared performance and accountability is built on a belief in people—in their willingness to grow, change, and make decisions that are best for the well-being of the whole. It is also built on an understanding of how engagement contributes to risk and reward. This must always be considered from two vantage points: the individual and the organizational. If the organization is divided into silos, frustration increases the risk that people will remain isolated within them. If the outer chaos triggers fear-based reactions, Low Road behaviors will likely increase the risk that others will react similarly.

Organizations that assess risk and reward from both an individual and an organizational perspective bring into focus the opportunities for greater performance and accountability.

In summary, every organization is filled with trapped potential. Performance and accountability for organization-wide results improve when:

Purpose is both meaningful and actionable.	*What organizational possibilities for collaborative action do you see?*
Connections unleash potential across related work.	*Where do individuals and functions need to work more effectively across organizational boundaries to improve shared accountability and collective performance?*
We make **quality trade-off decisions**, decisions that can make or break the bottom line.	*If you could engage a cross-functional team to improve one area of the business from a customer's perspective what would it be? What trade-off decisions need to be made?*

Differences, disruptions, and disconnects are seen as opportunities for innovation and improvement.	*Where do you see an opportunity to address differences and disconnects that would lead to improved results and relationships?*
A **strong sense of belonging** at work exists to support personal and organizational success.	*If you could create an environment in which people and performance were guaranteed to thrive, what first steps would you take and why? How would you begin?*

The Five Decisions framework gives organizations:

- A way to see how boundaries are at work to support or undermine results
- A method to engage people and their expertise in support of organization-wide results
- An opportunity for leaders to continuously discover new ways to improve their impact on people and performance.

Whether you choose to do this work yourself or invite Partnership Advantage to help, using the Five Decisions will give you a new vantage point on an age-old challenge—how to address the tension between functional excellence and organization-wide engagement. Once you understand how boundaries tend to divide work into separate and isolated parts, you can engage people to better understand the connections that need to be established to drive organization-wide performance and accountability in support of any strategic initiative.

This is how organizations do more with more.

When ROI for any strategic change depends upon cross-functional thinking, decision making, and action, engagement across areas of expertise is a challenge that must be met. With the Five Decisions approach, change management takes on a new meaning. The focus is on what has to change in the day-to-day thinking, decision making, and action to leverage distinct areas of expertise to deliver intended overall results. Change management also takes on a new role—engaging people to find and unleash connections that can transform silos into solutions that serve organization wide results, and the relationships that matter to them.

If you would like us to help put your organization on the path to performance and accountability, please contact us at www.partnershipadv.com. Partnership Advantage can provide Five Decisions support services to help your organization create:

- More traction on intended results
- More commitment to work across areas of expertise
- More cross-functional initiative at all levels
- More momentum on what *really* matters.

Epilogue

Out beyond ideas of wrongdoing and rightdoing,
there is a field. I'll meet you there.

When the soul lies down in that grass,
the world is too full to talk about.

Ideas, language, even the phrase *'each other'*
doesn't make any sense.

—Rumi

Reading Rumi's words are a breath of fresh air in a desperate moment. Like that first gasp of air we take after being tossed beneath an ocean wave, finally finding the surface. This poem describes a very different world than the one we learn about on the news. On the contrary, in the face of our differences we draw lines that divide us into right and wrong, good and evil, winner and loser. Yet win or lose, all that we have accomplished is to remain divided by differences.

This book is about organizations. But it is also about us as leaders. It is about the power we each have to find and heal the differences that divide people and work that belong together. The central question in the book is this: What do we choose at the boundaries of our differences, and what difference does that make, to results and to relationships? This question applies to organizations of course. But it also applies to the world, our communities, and our personal lives.

Boundaries help to define our work and our identities. But they also divide us from others on whom our lives and our work depend.

The Five Decisions process is also about the power of belonging at work, and the importance of connections that form the foundation to any innovative or integrated operation. It is also about the power of isolation and despair.

It often takes a crisis before we see ourselves as connected. The moments and days following 9/11 were filled with poignant examples of this. For a few days we were all New Yorkers, bound by our collective grief. We gave our money, time, and some even gave their lives in attempt to save perfect strangers. But our sense of connection and solidarity was fragile, and quickly gave way to isolation, alienation, and even violence.

This book is based on three beliefs:

1. Relationships are all we have. We experience life in and through our relationships with others, with our work, and with the larger world. We come to know who we are when we witness our beliefs and our values in action.

2. Healing our relationships, and our world, begins with

the courage to see and address the contradictions in our own lives. We cannot do for others what we cannot do for ourselves.

3. Work is a great learning laboratory for our lives. What is evoked at the boundary of our differences is an expression of who we are. What we choose is an expression of who we are becoming.

A number of years ago I had the pleasure of working with Ms. Shabazz—the eldest daughter of Malcolm X—as facilitators in a 4 day leadership retreat. The room was transfixed as she began her remarks with a profound question:

"What if we could begin with our barriers down?"

Ms. Shabazz was five years old on the day she witnessed her father's assassination. Her words, like Rumi's, issued the ultimate invitation, confrontation and call to action—to explore our own humanity, and how it gets expressed in and through our relationships. To transform barriers into boundaries that connect and restore.

This is perhaps the ultimate test of our leadership capacity. The fulcrum of development is awareness. The test is action.

* * *

About the Author

As the founder and CEO of Partnership Advantage, Tamara Sicard, PhD, helps organizations improve the quality of thinking, decision-making and action across the enterprise to reduce cycle time and increase quality, profitability and customer satisfaction.

Tammy's consulting philosophy focuses upon the person-at-work, understanding that only by effectively engaging and developing people will an organization be able to unleash performance and accountability. Her areas of expertise include strategic planning, integration across work processes, leadership development, and creating culture change. She has facilitated international teams in the areas of product and process innovation, and in implementing global technology solutions.

Tammy has a Doctorate in Human and Organization Systems from Fielding Graduate University. She serves on the Board of Directors for Impact Giving, a women's collective giving organization. Prior to founding Partnership Advantage, Tammy spent seventeen years leading operations and staff functions for Fortune 100 and 500 corporations.

Made in the USA
San Bernardino, CA
27 May 2016